D0804813

Dear Parent:

Your child's love of reading starts here!

Every child learns to read in a different way and at his or her own speed. Some go back and forth between reading levels and read favorite books again and again. Others read through each level in order. You can help your young reader improve and become more confident by encouraging his or her own interests and abilities. From books your child reads with you to the first books he or she reads alone, there are I Can Read Books for every stage of reading:

SHARED READING
Basic language, word repetition, and whimsical illustrations, ideal for sharing with your emergent reader

BEGINNING READING
Short sentences, familiar words, and simple concepts for children eager to read on their own

READING WITH HELP
Engaging stories, longer sentences, and language play for developing readers

READING ALONE
Complex plots, challenging vocabulary, and high-interest topics for the independent reader

I Can Read Books have introduced children to the joy of reading since 1957. Featuring award-winning authors and illustrators and a fabulous cast of beloved characters, I Can Read Books set the standard for beginning readers.

A lifetime of discovery begins with the magical words **"I Can Read!"**

Visit www.icanread.com for information
on enriching your child's reading experience.

I Can Read® and I Can Read Book® are trademarks of HarperCollins Publishers.

Pinkfong: Meet Pinkfong and Friends
Copyright © 2022 by The Pinkfong Company, Inc.
All rights reserved. Pinkfong™ is a trademark of The Pinkfong Company, Inc., registered or pending rights worldwide.
Printed in the United States of America.
No part of this book may be used or reproduced in any manner whatsoever without written permission except in the case of brief quotations embodied in critical articles and reviews. For information address HarperCollins Children's Books, a division of HarperCollins Publishers, 195 Broadway, New York, NY 10007.
www.icanread.com

Library of Congress Control Number: 2022938127
ISBN 978-0-06-327243-9

22 23 24 25 26 LBM 10 9 8 7 6 5 4 3 2 1 ❖ First Edition

My First SHARED READING

I Can Read!

Meet Pinkfong and Friends

HARPER

An Imprint of HarperCollinsPublishers

This is Pinkfong.

Pinkfong is a pink fox.

Pinkfong lives in a
magical world.

Pinkfong has magical
powers.
Pinkfong can make
wishes come true!

Pinkfong loves making magic
but loves adventures more!

Do you want to meet
some of Pinkfong's friends?

Nini is Pinkfong's
best buddy.
This little cat has big eyes.
Nini's fur is super soft.

Nini is a funny cat
who loves to dance!

It's time to meet Mo!
Mo is round and fluffy.
Mo will go wherever
Nini goes.
They are best friends!

Mo always sits
on Nini's head.
It makes Mo feel safe.
Mo also loves to sleep!
Night night, Mo!

When these three
are together,
they can do anything!

But Pinkfong has even
more friends!
Want to meet them?
Then let's go!

This is Baby Monkey!
He loves ba-na-na-na-nas!
Baby Monkey likes to dance,
too!

Mommy and Daddy
love bananas!
Grandma and Grandpa
love bananas!
Everyone loves bananas!

Beep! Beep! Vroom! Vroom!
Baby Car loves a good race.
Come take a spin!

Baby Car and his family
love a good dance party.
But be sure to wear
your seat belt!
It can get bumpy.

Now let's meet Baby T-Rex!
No need to worry.
He may have sharp teeth,
but T-Rex won't bite.

Say hello to the T-Rex
family!
They may look a bit scary,
but they just want
to have fun!
Time for a roar party!

Have you ever seen
a dancing penguin?
Let's learn the penguin
dance!

First, wiggle both flippers.

Then, shake both feet.

Next, nod your head.

Finally, turn around.

That's the penguin dance!

These chilly penguins love to show friends their dance moves.

Let's all do the penguin
dance!

The wheels on the bus
go round and round!
Say hello to the bus family!

Pinkfong and friends enjoy
seeing the sights of the city!

The bus family will take you on amazing adventures! Make sure you hold on!

And don't worry about
missing the bus.
There's a bus for everyone!
Let's hop on board
and get ready to explore!

Pinkfong sure has
a lot of friends!
But there is one more friend
Pinkfong wants us to meet.
This is a very special friend!
Who could it be?

It's you!

Pinkfong is so happy

to meet you.

Now we are all friends!